To my parents,
who used to take me around
National Trust properties as a child,
and I've never looked back.
PA

For the Jolly Boys, my Fellow Men at Arms.
JL

First published in the UK in 2017 by Nosy Crow Ltd
The Crow's Nest, 14 Baden Place,
Crosby Row, London, SE1 1YW, UK

The words 'The National Trust' and the oak leaf logo are registered trademarks of
National Trust for England, Wales and Northern Ireland used under licence from
National Trust (Enterprises) Limited (Registered Company Number 01083105).

Nosy Crow and associated logos are trademarks and/or
registered trademarks of Nosy Crow Ltd

Text copyright © Philip Ardagh, 2017
Illustrations © Jamie Littler, 2017

The right of Philip Ardagh and Jamie Littler to be identified as the author
and illustrator respectively of this work has been asserted by them in accordance
with the Copyright, Designs and Patents Act 1988.

A CIP catalogue record for this book will be available from the British Library

Printed and bound in the UK by Clays Ltd, St Ives Plc

Papers used by Nosy Crow are made from wood grown in sustainable forests.

ISBN: 978 0 85763 901 1

www.nosycrow.com

Day 1

My name is John Drawbridge and I now live at Widemoat Castle. I am filled with such happiness that I walk around with the biggest and widest of grins in Christendom[1]!

The only person I have seen with a wider grin is the Fool[2], a man who strolleth about with a pig's bladder on a stick.[3] (And he is a professional.)

---

1   The parts of the world then ruled by Christians from Europe
2   A sort of clown employed by the owner of the castle to entertain him and his guests.
3   A pig's bladder could be blown up to make the only kind of balloon you could get in medieval times.

This castle is a place of much wonderment and

Wow!

It hath towers and dungeons, battlements and kennels. I did not use to live in such a beauteous place. I was sent here to learn to be a knight. How wondrous is that? Of course, I will not get to become a knight in the blinking of a bat's eye. I am what is called a page in training which, the truth be told, meaneth that I am already a page but know not exactly what I am doing AND am earning a penny a day for it!

I am learning my skills
and duties on my feet.
And on my bottom
(because training to
be a page one getteth
knocked over quite a bit).
When I have become one
of Widemoat Castle's
best pages there hast
ever been, I shall then
get promoted to a
squire in training.[4]

---

4   A squire carried his knight's shield and weapons, looked after his
    horse, carried his messages, and ran his errands, whilst acting as his
    apprentice and learning is ways. A page had to learn all the basics
    before being able to have THAT honour.

And then, when people marvel mightily at what a truly magnificent squire I have become, I shall be dubbed a KNIGHT. ★Clappeth!★ ★Cheereth★ Thank you. (Well, that be my plan, anyway. And it will take many years.)

Because coming to this castle of wonderment is

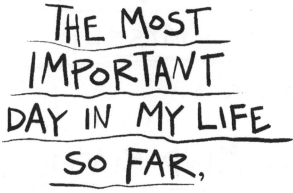

THE MOST
IMPORTANT
DAY IN MY LIFE
SO FAR,

it is my plan to keep a diary of great secret. There be one teeniest of teeny problems, however. Few, if any, people of my age – or any age – can read or write, so I am writing this within my head.[5]

---

5   And not in QUITE the way someone from medieval times would have written OR spoken. This is one of the advantages of mindingreading: it translates the original words into something more FUN.

This meaneth that

ANYONE
READING THIS
OTHER THAN
MYSELF

is, most likely, a

- MIND-READER. -

Most strange, is it not?

For this must mean

Let us commence!

Day 3

My brother Hubert ran
into me today, which
was about as welcome
as the finding of a dead
rat in the beef sauce[6]. Our
parents are Sir Norman
and Lady Drawbridge.
You can guess which is
which. (Clue: Do not try
calling my father 'Lady'
anything unless you find
pleasure in being held upside-down by your
ankles.)

It is not the son of just *anyone* who can train
to be a knight. You have to come from a good
and noble family. (And families do not come
more good and noble than the Drawbridges.)

★Gloweth with pride★

---

6   Without fridges to store meat in, it went off very quickly. The bad
    taste could be disguised with rich sauces.

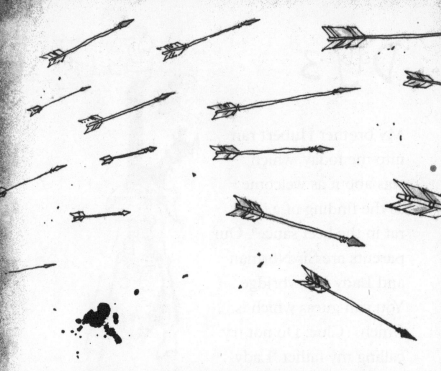

It matters not how good Thomas the miller's son is at riding[7] and fighting and firing homemade arrows (which he be). He can never be more than a miller's son. I do not say this be a good or a bad thing. It is simply a fact. (And Thomas doth bake the most excellent of breads, if thou like it black and crispy and tasting of burnt tree bark.)

---

7   Thomas would have borrowed his father's work horse. Only the rich and nobles rode the fast horses.

Hubert – *Booeth and Hisseth!* – is my *elder* brother, so he came here to Widemoat Castle a few years in advance of me. It pleased me, at first, for it meant that the layabout was out of the way and not being

A BIG
BROTHER
OF MUCH
ANNOYANCE

at home. (If you have an annoying brother or sister, multiply such causing of annoyance by one hundred and you shall merely begin to form an idea of just how annoying Hubert be.)[8]

---

8   A page was taught very basic maths along with some reading and writing.

Soon after he had gone, however, it occurred to me that this meaneth that he is likely to become a knight BEFORE ME. And this is so very *wrong*. Hubert becoming a knight is like a gong-farmer becoming king![9] I would laugh if I did not want to burst into tears and bury Hubert up to his neck in the dung of horses[10] (for he once did that very thing to me)[11].

---

9   A gong-farmer - usually a boy - had the job of clearing human poo
    from cesspits and privies at night.
10 Horse poo. (Sorry!)
11 Big brothers have been the same throughout history.

This remindeth me of a

JOKE

most chucklesome:

> *ME:*
> *What is brown and ringeth like a bell?*

> *YOU:*
> *I do not know, Master John.*
> *What IS brown and ringeth like a bell?*

> *ME:*
> *Dung! (Doest thou get it?*
> *DUNG!)*

(Followed by
much laughter.)

When Hubert ran into me without[12] the castle stables in the courtyard – very much on purpose – he sent me flying. I nearly landed upon a man crouching behind a barrel, doing whatever it was that he was doing.[13]

12 Here 'without' means 'outside', not 'not having'.
13 Old chainmail was sometimes put in a barrel of sand which was then rolled around, causing the sand to rub off the rust.

Hubert then made much pretence of it being MY fault for being in the way. He made more fuss than the man I landed upon, who simply scuttled away before I even caught so much as a glimpse of his face. During our time here, I very much hope that my brother and I see as little of each other as two moles that burrow in opposite directions.

Day 8

The Great Hall is by far the biggest room in the castle and is the centre of castle life. 'Tis here that most of us sleep at night. We sleep not in beds. Beds are for My Lord and Lady. The servants sleep upon straw on the floor of the hall, and the dirty straw is cleared away each morning. We squires and pages sleep upon a pallet or a trundle or, if less lucky, a straw mat. Old Sir Jack Olde – more on him another day – sayeth that one of the good things about so many people sleeping in the same place is that, on cold nights such as this, the heat from all those bodies helpeth to warm up the whole room. But this maketh not up for the snoring and mutterings and the elbowing for space. The tapestries[14] that hang from the cold, stone walls not only help to give a grand appearance but also help to keep the place a little warmer.

---

14 Tapestries often showed hunting scenes with lords and ladies on horseback and maybe a stag or wild boar between the trees.

The windows in the hall hath most impressive shutters. I think it will take me a goodly while to become used to sleeping in such a huge space with so many others.

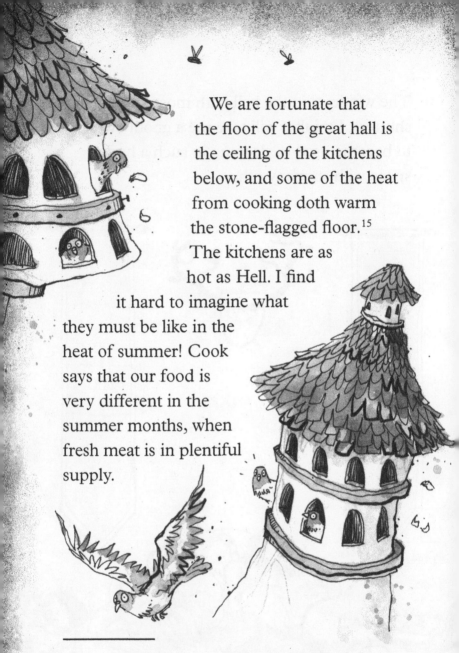

We are fortunate that
the floor of the great hall is
the ceiling of the kitchens
below, and some of the heat
from cooking doth warm
the stone-flagged floor.[15]
The kitchens are as
hot as Hell. I find
it hard to imagine what
they must be like in the
heat of summer! Cook
says that our food is
very different in the
summer months, when
fresh meat is in plentiful
supply.

---

15   In summer months, whole animals were spit-roasted in front of huge
     open fires.

With spring not yet upon us, the only fresh meat comes from pigeons from the dovecotes[16], otherwise we have to make do with dried meat – sometimes gone bad and cooked in herbs to disguise the gruesome taste ⋆Yerch!⋆ – or salted and smoked fish. Cook says that in deepest winter, when snow lieth upon the ground, that I would be grateful to be working in such warmth, but I cannot imagine ever getting used to such heat. Hubert, who sweats at the effort of frowning when he thinketh too hard, would melt into a useless blob were he not one already! (Sometimes I find myself chuckling at my own wit.)

---

16   Pigeons and doves were kept in dovecotes to look elegant and pretty and pleasing. And to cook and eat.

Day 9

The castle is such a different place by night.
By day, the windows offer sufficient light for us
to learn our duties and undertake our tasks. (In
other words: we can *see*.) After dark – besides
the Great Hall if there is feasting or the kitchen
with its great fire – much of the place is in
almost complete blackness. I look forward to
a full moon. Some areas are lit with torches.[17]
There also be candles but these be precious
and, of course, for the use of Lord and Lady
Widemoat and their more important guests.

Tonight, I was given an unlit candle stub in
the dark and, mistaking it for a piece of food, I
ate it! My face was so hot with embarrassment
that I am much surprised that it did not glow
red and light up the room! It would have been
more embarrassing if anyone had been able to

---

17   Not torch as in a battery-operated flashlight but as in a burning
      torch in a sanction/bracket on a wall.

see my stupidity.[18] If my brother were ever to find out, it would not be worth my living. Whilst fumbling in the dark, I heard hushed voices not far from me. I'm sure I heard the word "attack!" and half-expected a prank from my fellow pages, were it not for the fact that at least one of the voices I heard was an adult's. (That candle stump, by the by, did not taste *too* bad.)[19]

---

18   Unlike nowadays, where we take heating and lighting for granted, much of what could be done in medieval times was determined by daylight, with less activity in the darker, winter months.

19   Most candles were made from tallow (melted down animal fat) with a rush for a wick.

Day 12

The two fellow pages in training with whom I spend most time are Martin and Cadwallon. We are of much similar ages and they have been at the castle but a short while longer than me. The two are very different. Martin has fair hair, as do I, and is smaller than me. Cadwallon is from across the border in Wales and looks most foreign to my English eyes. His own eyes are as black as his hair and his hair is as black as his eyes, which means: MOST black. He speaketh English with an accent as well as speaking Welsh, his own tongue. We English were once at war with Wales but it is now part of the kingdom. That is not to say that all the Welsh are grateful for this fact. My father hath talked of 'rumblings' in the past, with the occasional uprising or rebellious act in this day and age. Cadwallon insisteth, however, that his father is a chief who hath always sided with the English and our king. (I should hope so, or why would he be allowed to train here at the castle?)

He claims his family also liveth in an ancient castle, high on a Welsh hill. This is so that it can be seen from many miles distance, as a symbol of authority, and also so that those within his castle can see for many miles when on the lookout for any approaching enemy.[20]

When Cadwallon said "enemy" he looked at me with his dark black eyes as though he had forgotten for a moment that we are on the same side. Or, at least, are *supposed* to be. Mist rose from his mouth in the cold air, like the smoke from the nostrils of a mighty Welsh dragon.

---

20 This was common practice. Castles were meant to look impressive. You didn't mess with its owner and get off lightly.

As for the other page, Martin, did I mention that he hath a VERY big nose? I have now. And it deserveth a very big mention, it being so very, very large in the nose department.

Day 13

Widemoat Castle impresseth me more as each day passeth. It is owned by Lord Widemoat, who also owneth the land further than I can see. (And my mother – Lady Drawbridge – says that I have the eyes of a hawk[21].) At the moment trees are bare but soon the leaves will grow as the weather warms.

---

21   You can find out more about hawks on page 80.

The land was given to Widemoat's father
by the King for helping him win some great
battle (with much stomping of horses' hooves,
clashing of swords, firing of arrows, and great
quantities of mud and blood).

Lord Widemoat was himself in many battles but doth no such fighting nowadays. I have seen him about the castle. He is of impressive age and as round as the barrels in which he keeps his ale.[22] When he shall die, the castle and lands will pass to Sir William, his eldest son, who will become the *new* Lord Widemoat. (William hath an older sister, Isabella, but her being a *she*, she shall inherit nothing.[23])

COMING SOON:
A new YOUNGER,
SLIMMER,
MORE ACTIVE
Lord Widemoat.

---

22 In Medieval times people drank ale which, unlike later beer, did not contain hops. Barrel-makers were called coopers after the word 'cupa', Latin for barrel.

23 This was why nobles – including kings – wanted to be sure to have at least one son.

Like many an important family, the Widemoats have their own coat of arms. Today, we were shown the Widemoat coat of arms on a tapestry.[24] Each part hath its own special name. I cannot yet read, but was told that the writing along the bottom spelleth out BENE PUGNATE NEC LUTUM TIMETE which is Latin[25] for: "FIGHT WELL AND DON'T WORRY ABOUT GETTING MUDDY!" It used to be the battle cry of Lord Widemoat but, I am told, it took so long to shout that he often ended up with mud in his mouth – thrown up by horses' hooves – and was unable to finish his sentence.

We Drawbridges also have our own coat of arms. Our motto is: "Good Manners. Good-Looking. Good luck!" My father once explained that a coat of arms began life as a coat WITHOUT arms. (Which maketh about

---

24 One of the most famous tapestries of all is The Bayeaux Tapestry, depicting the events surrounding the Battle of Hastings in 1066. In truth, it is not a tapestry at all. It is embroidered. Tapestries are woven, embroidery is sewn.

25 The language originally of the Romans in ancient Rome. The Bible was written in Latin in medieval times, and priests spoke Latin.

as much sense as my idiot brother usually does.) It was worn upon a knight's armour so that, in battle, each side might know for whom the other was fighting.

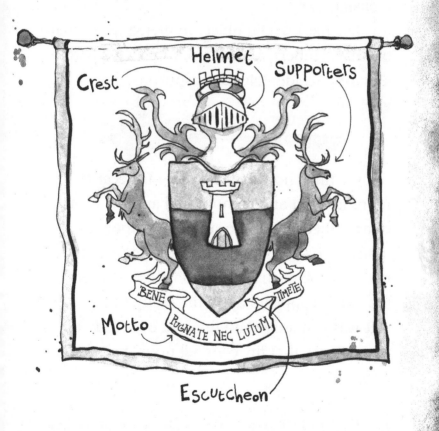

Without such a coat, bearing their lord's emblem, a helmeted knight in armour looks very like any other helmeted knight in armour. Before the idea of a coat of arms, brother could be bashing brother upon the head without realising it.

(Not that I would object to giving mine own brother, Hubert, a clunk upon the head with a mace[26] accidentally-upon-purpose once in a while.)

Over time, however, the designs became more fanciful and complicated and the coats of arms became of the style I saw upon the tapestry. Knights still often wear coats of arms and the designs upon their shields matcheth that which appears upon the escutcheon.

It was just as we had finished our study of the tapestry that my eyes fell upon a sight most unusual.

---

26 A spiked iron ball on the end of a wooden handle. A spiked iron ball on the end of a chain attached to a wooden handle is a morning-star.

’Twas

A PAIR
OF FEET

sticking out beneath another
tapestry on the far wall, of a
wild-boar hunt in a forest[27]!!!

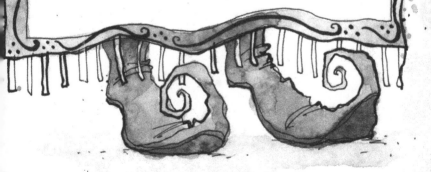

---

27   There were many wild boar in the woods in medieval times, which
      noblemen would hunt for sport and for food.

I was about to speak out when Old Sir Jack Olde barked some new instructions. He be the man in charge of us pages and we do not stop to question or to argue (but more of him anon[28]). I nudged Martin in the ribs and pointed at the feet and he raised his eyes in surprise. We had to leave the room but – as sure as God made unicorns[29] – I will recognise those shoes if I ever see them again.

---

28   Anon means later, as in "see you anon", meaning "see you later".

29   The unicorn was – and still is – one of the supporters on the British monarchy's coat of arms. The other is a male lion.

Day 14

Yesterday, we newest pages were shown farther about the castle by Old Sir Jack Olde. He seemeth as old as his name suggesteth. His skin appeareth so tough and leathery, I am surprised he needeth armour! I can imagine arrows bouncing off him, with a TWANG most satisfying.

We did not go within every room within the castle for:

1. there be such a great number of them.
2. some of them be PRIVATE.

We did not get to see inside the oubliette[30] either, for the simple reason that it hath neither door nor window and is not lit. This sorry place is a dungeon for prisoners who will never see the light of day again. They are dropped through a hole in the roof which is then shut off by an iron grille (through which I peered but saw nothing). They may be enemies of the castle but I cannot help but feel sorry for them. Sir Jack told us that, in some other castles nearer the sea, at high tides their oubliettes sometimes flood... I fear this is not so that the prisoners might wash[31] or have a nice little splash about, but so that they will drown.

Widemoat Castle hath rooms both BIG and small. One such variety of small room is the garderobe. It hath a proper toilet in it. It hath a nice smooth wooden seat (avoiding splinters) -- with a hole within it -- on which to rest one's

---

30   Oubliette comes from the French meaning 'to forget'. Prisoners were usually put in here then forgotten about. In other words, they were left to die.

31   People rarely washed or bathed. Even the rich did not have bath tubs, let alone bathrooms.

behind. I was testing this out (by sitting on it but with my hose[32] still up) when Cadwallon, the black-eyed page from wildest Wales, let out a mighty noise pretending that it was made by my bottom. There was much laughter until Old Sir Jack clipped him around the ears[33]. Cadwallon looketh most different when he smileth.

---

32 Trousers.
33 In medieval times, it wasn't seen as rude to talk about 'bodily functions'. Some road names used back then would be faaaaaaar too rude to use today. Cadwallon got a clip around the ear for messing about when he should be learning, not for the actual noise he made!

Old Sir Jack informed me that when he was a boy, people used to store clothes in garderobes to keep the moths from them.[34] Nowadays, there be no clothes[35] there but a bowl of dried herbs in this one, disguising any nasty smells with pleasing ones.

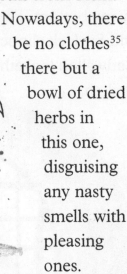

(It would take a barrel-full of herbs to cover up the smells my big brother Hubert maketh. But, having said that, no moth would stand a chance against his thunder.)

There be some torn-up squares of parchment

---

34 Moths – whose larvae ate clothes – were thought not to like the smell of pee and neither were fleas so a garderobe was supposed to guard the robes against moths and fleas!

35 The clothes were kept in the wardrobe: 'ward' meaning to protect and 'robe' referring to the clothes.

to use as paper. It is an improvement on using moss and leaves. The waste – that be the polite word for it, anyway – slideth down a chute and out into the moat. What could be better?[36] I saw Martin slip one such scrap of parchment beneath his shirt when Old Sir Jack's attention was elsewhere. When I later asked him what he wanted it for, he said: "What doest thou think I wanted it for? For wiping my own behind!"

Pardon ME for asking!

Old Sir Jack bade me look down the chute and I noticed an iron grille halfway down.

"Prithy[37], what is that for?" I enquired.

"What dost thou think it for?" he asked.

"To stop people falling down the toilet?" I suggested.

"To stop birds flying up it?" suggested Martin.

"To stop people climbing up it!" Olde Sir Jack replied.

---

36   Just one excellent reason for not swimming in the moat.

37   The word 'prithy' is a shortening of 'pray thee' and simply means 'please'

YES. Those are the very words that passed his lips:

TO STOP PEOPLE CLIMBING UP IT.

"Who would wish to climb up a toilet?" asked Cadwallon, his black eyes flashing. I thought this a good question because even my idiot brother Hubert would not choose to do such a thing.

"Enemy attackers trying to sneak into the castle," said Old Sir Jack Olde. "Each garderobe hath such a grille. Well, all but one, but that soon will be repaired."

ZOUNDS!!![38] I would not want to be given either of those jobs: to climb down to make such a repair or to climb up to attack!

---

[38] A shocked exclamation, actually a shortening of 'God's wounds!' referring to the wounds inflicted on Jesus when he was crucified, according to the Christian faith.

Day 17

Today I first laid eyes on Lady Gertrude, the daughter of Lord Brian and Lady Pikestaff. She was sent here to Widemoat Castle when she was six to learn from the Lady Widemoat the ways of managing a household[39].

---

39 The lady of the castle would often run the household, instructing the steward, and even acting on her lord's behalf when he was away. Young noble girls were sent from their own homes to be trained by them.

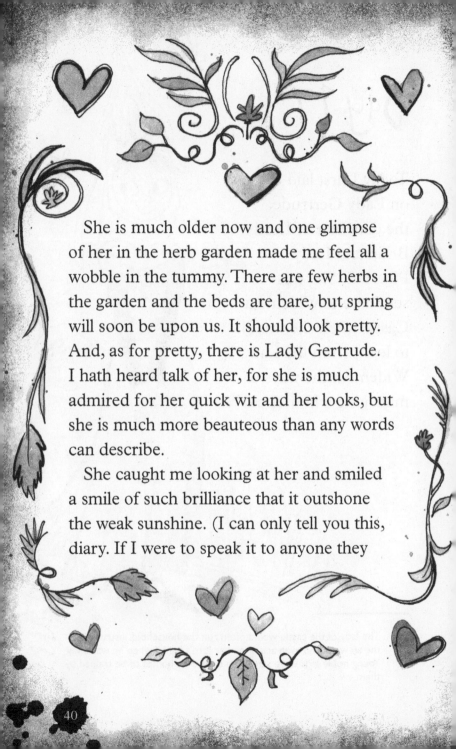

She is much older now and one glimpse
of her in the herb garden made me feel all a
wobble in the tummy. There are few herbs in
the garden and the beds are bare, but spring
will soon be upon us. It should look pretty.
And, as for pretty, there is Lady Gertrude.
I hath heard talk of her, for she is much
admired for her quick wit and her looks, but
she is much more beauteous than any words
can describe.

She caught me looking at her and smiled
a smile of such brilliance that it outshone
the weak sunshine. (I can only tell you this,
diary. If I were to speak it to anyone they

would taunt and tease me until I was redder than a boar's head at Christmas[40].) I was about to leave when she asked me my name.

ME. My name!

I suddenly found that I had almost forgot it… But I remembered just in time. I tried to reply, "John Drawbridge" with my voice as deep as possible to give a most manly impression.

---

40 In medieval times, the finest Christmas meal was not turkey or goose but a boar's head. And the boar had to be hunted before its head could be cooked for the Christmas feast. It was often served with an apple in its mouth to keep the shape of its jaw and to show off its teeth and tusks. Once cooked, the head looked very red.

She laughed. I imagine that is what the laughter of an angel would sound like if an angel heard a really good joke. Now my toes were tingling.

"I like your hennin, my lady," I said, pointing at her extremely large hat[41].

"Why, thank you, Master Drawbridge," she replied, her voice like clear running water (and I do not mean she dribbled). Then she asked me about my training. I would have stayed longer had not Cadwallon appeared at my side, to inform me that Old Sir Jack Olde was looking for me. It is very much my hope that the Lady Gertrude and I do meet again at the soonest.

---

41 Fashions changed but the hennin was by far the tallest and most pointy hat.

Day 22

Ouch! These past few days, I have been learning how to charge with a lance upon horseback. Rather than charging against a fellow page, I have to try to hit the tip of my lance against a target upon a contraption called a quintain.[42]

---

42 Unlike a knight, who is charging at another knight with a lance charging at him from the opposite direction.

When I knock the target, a sack swingeth round. The first time, it knocked me clean off my horse. And the second. Not the third. But the fourth. Some days be better than others. Today I am feeling most battered and bruised. I am better at it than Martin, but lack the skill of Cadwallon, who hath proved himself to be most artful at this task. You can tell when I have had quintain practice, for I must stagger about cross-eyed for a while. I have been told that I look like a horse drunk on rotten apples.

Day 23

A great crowd of different sorts of people with different jobs and duties live and work in the castle[43]. There are SO many, I wonder if I shall ever meet them all. Some faces I see often – such as those who work in the kitchen from whence I collect dishes[44] to serve at table – others on occasion, then there must be those I have yet to meet or may never.

---

43   Apart from the lord's wife, daughters and a few ladies-in-waiting, every single person living in a castle – whatever their job – were men. A washerwoman would have come in to wash clothes but she wouldn't stay. If any of the men working there chose to marry, they'd have to leave the castle and the lord's payroll to set up on their own.

44   Dishes of food. Not empty ones!

As well as Lord and Lady Widemoat and their knights and squires and pages, there is every kind of servant you can think of, from the cooks in the kitchen to the kennel boy who actually sleepeth in the kennels with the hunting dogs! His name is Doug and he smelleth much of dog. I am sure he even barketh at me on occasion. (He also whistleth in the most untunely of manners, causing much aching of the ears.) There be the soldiers who guard the castle. There be the armourers who look after the armour and a falconer who looks after and trains falcons for hunting.

There be candlemakers, and clerks, grooms and valets, but there also be others with less obvious job titles:

FLETCHERS make arrows for the archers.

He knoweth all one needs to know to craft the very finest of arrows.

OSTLERS look after the orses. (Pray, forgive me. I mean _H_orses.)

A horse is the single most important thing to a knight. More so than his armour and finery. Without horses a man cannot travel great distances nor attack at such speed. And, without his mount,[45] he would be little more than a glorified foot soldier. The Chief Ostler is Harry Oats. It is most difficult to tell him and the horses apart without counting his legs, so horsey is his countenance.

---

45   Horse.

BLACKSMITHS make horseshoes for horses. (Who else would they make them for?) Sam, the apprentice smith[46], is forever hitting his thumb or burning it upon hot metal. Unlike FARRIERS, who just make shoes for horses, Magnus (the castle blacksmith) also maketh everything from door hinges to chains to the iron on the rims of a wagon's wheels to stop the wood from wearing.

Lord Widemoat even hath a MINSTREL whose job it is to compose songs about his lordship's brave and chivalrous acts[47]. These are then performed at banquets to impress his guests. (I have had the good fortune to listen to them on a number of occasions but do now feel that I've heard them quite enough.)

Gather round for thee to hear me,
Gather round, one and all.
Pray thee come and stand thee near me,
In this great and mighty hall,
And I'll tell thee a fine tale
Of a lord of highest note:
That brave and glorious, mighty fighter
Your lord and master, Lord Widemoat.

---

47 Chivalry was a knightly code for behaving with honour.

Charles the Minstrel playeth the lute[48] and practiceth by singing to the doves. This afternoon, I witnessed Cadwallon asking him to play a particular Welsh tune, close to his  heart, and Charles pulled such a face that it caused the nearest dove to fly from its perch in fright. He – the minstrel, not the frightened bird – replied that he did not play *foreign* songs (despite the fact that Wales now be part of our one kingdom). I felt a twinge of sadness for Cadwallon: away not only from his home but from his country.

---

48 A stringed instrument about the size of a smallish guitar.

Day 26

For me, the most pleasing part of the castle is the drawbridge, and this be not simply because Drawbridge is my family name. It is because it be such an ingenious device! Today, at long last and after many days of asking most politely, Old Sir Jack let me and Martin help to raise and lower it together, once he had gained permission from the Captain of the Guard.

I have discovered that Martin is the son of Lord and Lady de Conk, which explaineth the bigness of his nose. I should have thought of it previously! (I did mention his nose, dear diary, did I not?

The ENORMITY

of it?)

The de Conk family is known to my own family and its members have the nickname 'Big Nose' because of the great size of their noses. I am recently affeared that Martin may poke out mine eye with it if he suddenly turns to me. It is lucky that I am taller than he. We have become better and better friends by the day, unlike Cadwallon the Welsh boy. He is friendly enough when we are training and sometimes is most naughty and amusing. When we are not training, however, he keepeth himself very much to himself. Sometimes I hear him mutter in his native tongue. It sounds most foreign to mine English ears and as if he be casting a spell. When he frowneth, he looketh like a demon from a story!

Working the drawbridge was hard and Martin and I developed much sweatiness. (He is clearly stronger than I, but he lacketh my stunning Drawbridge looks.)

Here is how the drawbridge worketh:

WINCH

PULLEY

CHAIN

DRAWBRIDGE

PIVOT

MOAT

When up, the wooden bridge is a great and mighty door. When lowered, it reacheth across part of the moat to a small island, upon which sits a tower. This tower is the barbican which, in times of DANGER, is bristling with more of Lord Widemoat's soldiers than there be bristles on a wild boar, ready to defend the castle

TO THE DEATH.

(Dramatic, is it not?)

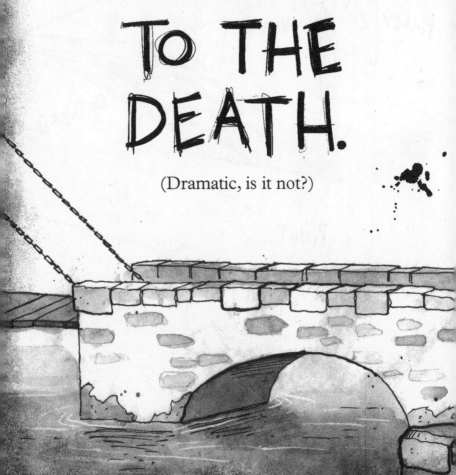

To one side of the barbican is a fixed wooden bridge which runneth *all* the way across the rest of the moat to dry land.

Old Sir Jack took us up to the top of the barbican to look down upon the bridge below. The sky was grey and it was gently raining. "Guess why it was built alongside to the castle, instead of going in a straight line with the lowered drawbridge?" he asked.

Martin suggested it might have something to do with fishing, but there be no fish in the moat. The water is stagnant and the stench coming from it is almost overpowering. I am

told that, on hot days, the smell is worse still.[49]
I am not, therefore, much looking forward to
the summer! With Martin having a nose of
such magnitude, I have little doubt that it has
room enough to store even greater amounts of
smellage than my own! Martin likes fish. I have
seen him stop and watch them in the ponds.[50]
In truth, he liketh most animals. He hath a pet
rat whom he hath named Rat.[51] I do not think
this particularly original.

---

49   Most moats were filled with stagnant (rather than running) water
     which made them rather smelly. Add to that the sewage from the
     garderobes and you can see why the stank.

50   Many castles had fishponds. Though they were often made to look
     attractive, they were also 'living larders'. The fish were bred to cook
     and eat. For religious reasons, the menu was fish on Fridays.

51   Rats were a real problem in castle store rooms and kitchens.

Cadwallon suggested that the bridge be parallel to the castle so that we might more easily see the coats of arms[52] worn by the arriving people so that we might know whether they are friend or foe[53].

"A good answer," said Old Sir Jack Olde, "but not the correct one."

Cadwallon muttered something beneath his breath which sounded to me like the clearing of the throat but would no doubt have meant something mighty rude to a fellow Welshman.

I knew the answer to the angling of the bridge but only because my elder brother Hubert had told me in the past. He is always one who likes to show off his great knowledge of very little. (He is such a hufty-tufty[54]). This was one of the rarest of times where something that he told me proved

USEFUL

---

52   See page 28.
53   Foe is another word for enemy.
54   a boaster

"If enemy soldiers be marching across a bridge that runneth alongside the castle wall, it is much easier for Sir Widemoat's soldiers to fire arrows and throw objects down upon them than if they be attacking face-on and are only one-man wide," I said.

"Thou art a clever lad," said Sir Jack and he gave me such a hearty slap upon the back that my teeth did rattle. I nearly toppled from the battlements into the stinking moat. (Martin laughed like a victorious cockerel[55].)

Here is what I meant by easier target:

---

55   In medieval times, two cockerels were often set to fight against each other – usually to the death – in the barbaric 'sport' of cock-fighting.

Day 32

This morning, Old Sir Jack had me run up one of the spiral staircases with a wooden sword, and bade me imagine I was attacking the castle. He had Martin come down the staircase with a wooden sword imagining he was defending it. This was doubly unfair. Firstly, I was worried that if his sword missed me his nose may not. (I jest.[56]) Secondly, coming down, he could wave his sword freely in his right hand, but mine was blocked by the pillar on the right as one goeth up.[57]

---

56   He means that he is jesting or making a jest. In other words: joking. (Hence the word jester.)

57   Most people are right-handed and, back then, most left-handed people would have been encouraged/forced to use their right, anyway.

Old Sir Jack informed us that the castle was deliberately built in such a way as an extra form of defence. Most ingenious! Unless thine enemy be left-handed, of course.[58] (And, yes, I found myself knocked to the ground, flat upon my bottom once AGAIN.) As Martin ran past me laughing, a scrap of parchment fluttered from his pocket: the piece he'd taken from the garderobe. I grinned and tucked it in my belt. Martin had written upon it. My reading is most basic but there was only one word: MEWS. That is the name of the castle cat, who hangeth around the kitchens. His job is to keep down the rats in the grain store so we are not allowed to feed him any titbits. (The idea being that, if he be hungry, he must kill a rat to feed.) I smiled to myself. Martin and his love of animals.

---

58   Left-handed people were often consider unlucky. The word 'left' comes from an Anglo Saxon word for 'weak'. Even the word sinister – meaning giving the impression that something is evil or harmful – comes from the Latin for pocket (which came to mean 'left' because the pocket was always on the left side of the toga).

Another more obvious castle defence, along with battlements and high, thick walls, be the

MURDER HOLES.

How splendid a name is that? Imagine that you have somehow managed to cross the fixed bridge, past the soldiers in the barbican and past the drawbridge. Now you find yourself face to face with the portcullis. 'Tis like a mighty iron-grid door.

Now imagine that you have managed to get past *THAT* – Heaven knows how – and thou art in the gatehouse.

Look up.

Do you see the stone ceiling?

Do you see the holes in that ceiling?

Too late!

For we are dropping boiling water, arrows, rocks, anything and everything upon you.[59]

Ha! Haah! Now you could not be any more dead no matter how hard you tried.

By the most remarkable piece of good fortune – praise be! – brother Hubert was walking through the gatehouse when we were investigating the holes with Old Sir Jack Olde from above. (I later discovered he had been sent on an errand to the barbican by his master, Sir Richard Kitchen.) This resulted in my being able to drop a few pebbles through the holes onto his head. He was most annoyed. Imagine how he felt when I dropped the chicken droppings!

---

59   People often talk about pouring boiling oil through murder holes, but this would have been wasteful and expensive.

He was FURIOUS, but his anger cannot have been any near as great as my generous feeling of SATISFACTION!

Day 43

This evening, at the grandest of banquets possible in these months – unlike the sumptuous feasts of summer[60] – something strange occurred. Banquets are held in the Great Hall. There is a high table around which the lords and ladies sit.

---

60   When food is in season, banquets would even include whole swans (with the feathers put back on after cooking).

This is upon a raised wooden platform so that the guests may see Lord and Lady Widemoat, who sit at the centre of the table, in their finery[61]. I have only fallen off the platform twice. Once was when I was avoiding Martin's nose as he dashed past me with an ale-flagon.[62] The second occasion was this very day when, I have no doubt, I was tripped. My knee still throbbeth.

Yes. I am as sure as I can be sure without actually being the other person to whom the foot belonged, that someone DELIBERATELY TRIPPED ME UP, though I am greatly puzzled – with much frowning – as to why. (If it had been my brother, I would not have given it a second thought other than my plotting my revenge, most likely with a mud pie.)

---

61   Finest clothes and jewels.
62   A flagon is like a large jug. These were usually ceramic (hardened clay), covered in a brightly coloured glaze.

Less important people sit at lower tables, most of which are made from huge wooden planks resting upon supports. Unlike the high table, these are not covered in a tablecloth. As well as a cloth of such dazzling white – at the start of the feast at least – the high table has a second, smaller table cloth placed upon it with a most colourful strip running down the middle. This, I am told, is called the sanap and it was upon the sanap that the servants place the choicest dishes.

Right before his lordship is placed the salt cellar. It is larger than the biggest goblet and is made of the finest silver. The nearer the one sitteth to the salt, the more important one is seen to be in the eyes of all others. Those 'below the salt' are of lesser importance. It is shaped like a fine ship.[63] I should like to see a real ship one day. Perhaps, as a knight, I shall set sail for the Holy Lands on a Crusade[64], though I did once feel seasick when floating upon a plank in a pond back home.

---

63 Many medieval salt cellars were decorated with motifs of the sea, perhaps because salt can be extracted from seawater. Humans need salt to survive.
64 The Crusades were 'Christian' military campaigns given the blessing of the Roman Catholic Church, often against Saracens (the word most often used by Europeans in medieval times for Muslims or followers of Islam).

A banquet is a noisy time with much talking and laughter, and much else besides. To show you like something you have eaten you should do a really loud BELCH. And when you have finished gnawing on a bone you should throw it on the floor for the dogs, who snap and yap to be the ones to win it. (It is, however, thought of as most rude to fart or to scratch a fleabite. And picking one's nose – or anyone else's nose for that matter – is the height of lower manners.) Also, although your plate – a trencher – is made of stale bread and soaketh up all the rich sauces, you should not eat it at the end of the meal, for the trenchers

are collected up and given to the poor.[65] (Though I did see a certain groom nibble at the corner of his.)

I take it upon myself to listen in on the gossip, at the same time as concentrating very hard upon my duties. (I heard talk of 'fresh rumblings of discontent' and of 'Welsh lords unhappy with our English king'. I also heard much excitement about Lord Widemoat's newest hawk with which he plans to hunt tomorrow.[66] I was so busy listening in on this last matter that I nearly spilt some ale upon Sir William Grant. He gave me a frown that was enough to cause one of the dogs at his feet to whimper. But it was not Sir William who put his boot in my path.

---

65 John isn't making up the belching, bone-throwing or stale-bread plates, however rude or crazy it may sound by today's standards. It's all true.

66 Birds were usually flown for 6 months during the winter, then rested for 6 months to allow them to moult – lose their old feathers and grow new ones – during spring and summer.

The honour for this ill-deed belongs to a visiting knight by the name of Sir Theobald Oakwood. He was also seated at high table, dressed in much finery, and using the finest of daggers[67]. He is the kind of man whose head is always tilted backward so as to have his nose in the air and to look down upon others. After he stuck out his foot and I tumbled from the dais, he gave a cruel laugh and called me "Foolish boy!" There was much apologising by the steward, who shooed me to the kitchen.

BUT IT WAS NOT MY FAULT.

---

67   People cut their food with their dagger and sometimes ate their food off the end of it. Forks were a much later invention and knives-and-forks just for eating with came even later still.

Though many hours have passed since then, my opinion of Sir Theobold has not changed: I like him not one bit.

That is not to say that my fall did not have its benefits too. Whilst lying on the floor, however briefly, I caught a glimpse of a very familiar pair of feet. Last seen sticking from the bottom of a tapestry. These feet did not belong to someone at high table but at the table to the right. Around this table sit the more important of Lord Widemoat's servants: his steward, Merrick, in charge of the whole household and the suchlike. I didn't have time to work out to whose legs the feet were attached and then to follow them to above table-height. But at least I now know that it was not some errand boy hiding that day but someone of more importance, if not actually noble. Most curious indeed.

Day 44

After yesterday's banquet, today His Lordship hath been showing off his latest hawk to his guests as he leads them on a hunt.

This was the reason for last night's banquet. My brother Hubert hath done me one of the greatest favours in his useless life. He awoke with such a stomach ache that he could barely groan let alone stand upon his own two feet. He was due to accompany his master, Sir Richard Kitchen, for whom he squires upon the hunt. Now a replacement had to be chosen from the pages, and Old Sir Jack chose ME. Martin said that he did not mind, which surprised me. He has a love of the falcons and spends what little time he can with them when the falconer allows. But he told me that he had a cold and runny nose. For anyone with a nose of such impressive size, I imagine his cold is most impressive also, with great waterfalls of runniness! I petty the poor woman who might nurse him.[68] Cadwallon was less pleased, and he muttered something which – to my English ears – sounded as if he were referring to me as a lucky, boar-headed boy with the breath

_____

68   Nursing the sick was one of the very few jobs in a castle carried out
      by women,

of a hundred onions. (Though, if the
truth be told, he may well have been
saying, "Oh bother!") His scowl
said it all however.

He was not best
pleased.

The falconer is a man named Fallow who knoweth all there is to know about birds of prey. He keeps them in two long, low buildings called mews. The word "prey" in birds of prey (falcons and the like) refers to their preying upon – attacking – smaller birds which are, in turn, their prey. It hath nothing to do with pray as in praying to God, as my idiot brother Hubert once insisted when pretending to know more than he does, as always.

The two main ways by which Fallow acquires new birds for the hunt are either by capturing in the wild when young, or rearing them from eggs. Either way, Fallow needs to train them. First off is the 'manning', where he simply getteth them used to humans. This is called Walking the Falcon. Fallow says that it be a very slow process and that he needeth the patience of St Kevin.[69] He weareth a thick glove upon the hand – a leather gauntlet – on which a bird perches. This comes as no

---

69   It is said that a bird laid her eggs on St Kevin's hand, so he held his arm in that position until the eggs had hatched, the birds grown up and flown the nest!

surprise for its talons be the weapons with which it hunts: razor-sharp and deadly.

Hood

Gauntlet

Bells

Rein

Purse (with 'rewards')

Fallow explained that he traineth a young bird to wear a hood over its eyes and a rein attached to its leg. With the hood removed but the rein still on, the young falcon then learneth to catch items thrown into the air by the falconer and to return with them to his gloved hand, in return for titbits. This way, over time, Fallow teacheth it to hunt for small birds in flight and return to his master or mistress.

We were talking in the mews as Fallow made final preparations. I was so distracted – fascinated by the way he handled each magnificent bird with such confidence and obvious affection – that I stumbled on an empty sack, half-covered by the straw scattered upon the hard-earth floor, and fell forward towards a perching bird. She made a shrill cry and flapped her wings but did not attempt to fly. Fallow spoke to her in soothing words.

"Careful, Master John!" he warned me, and I gave the most genuine of apologies. To have injured such a prize bird on the day of a hunt would have been a catastrophe!

I stood back then, and watched as Fallow gave birds to each member of Lord Widemoat's hunting party. He explained that the breed of bird showed the status of the man who hunted with it. And the ladies of the hunt each had their own Merlin[70].

King:	Gyr Falcon (male & female)
Prince:	Peregrine Falcon
Duke:	Rock Falcon (subspecies of Peregrine)
Earl:	Tiercel Peregrine
Baron:	Bastarde Hawk
Knight:	Saker
Squire:	Lanner
Lady:	Female Merlin
Yeoman:	Goshawk or Hobby
Priest:	Female Sparrowhawk
Holy water Clerk:	Male Sparrowhawk
Knaves, servants, children:	Kestrel

---

70   Not to be confused with the wizard Merlin from the legends of King Arthur, who probably wasn't a real person anyway.

GYR FALCON

PEREGRINE FALCON

SAKER FALCON

FEMALE MERLIN

SPARROWHAWK

There be many types of hunting, all of which Lord Widemoat greatly enjoys. He hunteth foxes, wild boar and wolves[71] but, according to Old Sir Jack Olde, has yet to successfully catch or kill a bear.[72] These are all men's sports, though, but with falconry, the ladies may too enjoy the hunt.

When I asked Fallow if people hath a chance to fly birds of a type other than their own, he looked deeply shocked.

"You could lose a hand for that!" he gasped.

"Their beaks and talons are that sharp?" I asked.

He shook his head. "That is not what I meanest, Master John," he said. "I mean that using a bird above thy social status is seen as an act of rebellion! A knight cannot fly a hawk,

---

71   Much of Britain was thick forest in medieval times and wolves were common. They could be a danger to travellers, particularly in the winter when food was more scarce.
72   Yes, there were bears in Britain back then.

nor a yeoman[73] a saker. The punishment is to have your hand chopped off!"

I shuddered. ★Gulp★ Some people do take their sport most seriously!!!

---

73   A yeoman owned a small piece of land, rather than working his master's land as a peasant or labourer, but was not gentry or noble. He would practice the longbow in case he was called on to fight by the local lord or the king.

Soon the hunting party was ready to depart, my running alongside Sir Richard Kitchen's horse.

I cannot report much of the day's actual sport, other than to say that the skies were filled with birds of prey of varying sizes and magnificence and many smaller birds fell victim to them. There was much excitement, conversation and laughter between Lord and Lady Widemoat and their noble followers and guests. I was kept busy running alongside Sir Richard, answering to his every whim. I felt I

served him well and he too seemed satisfied,
which made me proud... even if my feet did
end up sorer than something very sore indeed.

When we returned to the castle, Cadwallon
went out of his way not to ask me about the
day, and Martin emerged from a garderobe
looking far less red-nosed than I had feared he
might. (I had returned his scrap of dropped
parchment a few days previously and guess
that he must have used it for the smooooothest
wiping of his bottom!)

Day 55

I am exhausted from yet another day of training. The sun is brighter, the weather is warmer and I am sweatier still. But I am now completely settled into the working life of the castle. I am used to the fact that it be a community constantly under guard. Even when there is a banquet underway, the soldiers are ready just in case anyone be brave or foolish enough to try to attack the castle.

The castle guards have four main weapons: a pike staff, a

sword, a longbow and a crossbow.

I know full well why the castle windows are so very narrow. 'Tis for two important reasons:

1. Because no-one wanteth the wind whistling through them like it does through the gap in my big brother Hubert's front teeth.[74]

2. Because no-one wanteth attacking soldiers to be able to fire their arrows through windows and into the castle.

But I also now know why Widemoat Castle hath some ingenious cross-shaped windows, like this.

---

74   Apart, perhaps, from a window in a chapel, windows didn't have glass. Some had wooden shutters or drapes in front of them to keep out the cold. The word 'window' actually comes from the term 'wind hole'.

A longbow can be fired through the upright slit and the crossbow through the crossways one. This is indeed MOST ingenious, is it not? It is for this reason that they are called arrow slit windows, though this particular type doth take on the appearance of a Christian cross.

A long bow looks like a giant bow-and-arrow

A crossbow is a complicated piece of machinery.

The string be made of metal and be pulled tight and into place by means of a winch.

Sir Jack had two masters of the art demonstrate their skills, both more proud of their particular type of bow than the other. Alan de Witt fired the longbow, letting off a dozen arrows in the time it took the Sergeant at Arms[75] to fire one bolt.

Alan de Witt's arrows travelled slow and far

---

75   The Captain of the Castle Guard.

but the Sergeant's bolt
fired at incredible speed,
ripping through the
front of two of the
straw targets and
out of the back.

"It would do the same to a man," he told us with pride.

Cadwallon's black eyes glinted in fascination. He had showed a particular interest in the workings of the crossbow and was relieved when the Captain of the Guard said that we might each take a turn.

Another man, meanwhile, had appeared through an open doorway, and was pulling Alan de Witt's arrows from the target. He strode over to return them to his master. The top of his head looked as smooth as a metal helmet, but he had much frizziness of hair about the back and sides.

It was his shoes that really got my attention, though. For they were THE shoes.

Those shoes.

The ones last seen beneath the banquet table!

Day 58

This evening, Martin tried to squeeze through
a square hole in the thick metal grid which
is the lowered portcullis. He was watched
by myself and a small audience of laughing
soldiers, in the fading spring sunlight. He
informed them and me most assuredly that if
Rat (his rat) could fit through the smallest of
spaces, why should he not also? As we were
soon to discover, the reason why-not was
simple enough. It was because he would get
stuck. I wish I could say that it was his nose
which prevented him from squeezing through,
but that would be a falsehood.

Day 60

A good many days have passed since I laid eyes on the shoes of Tobias de Witt (for I now know that this be his name). He is, I have discovered, the older cousin of Alan, the longbowman, but acts as his assistant. Since Tobias's father died, he seems to have been at his wit's end and it is out of kindness that Baron Widemouth lets him live and work at the castle. Tobias's father was killed in a tavern brawl.

A tavern be a house in a town which hath given over a room or two to the selling of ale. It may also offer a bed for the night for a few weary travellers[76]. These are not places usually visited by the likes of the Widemoats or Drawbridges.

---

76 Early taverns were just ordinary houses. Over time, whole houses became taverns and, later, some were especially built for the purpose.

I do not know with whom Tobias de Witt's father fought, or what happened to the man who killed him, but I do know that Tobias has assisted his younger cousin, Alan, for many a year. There are different stories as to what the fight was about. Doug, the kennel boy, told me that it was an argument over a bone[77], but I think that unlikely. (Doug seems to love a good bone as much as do the dogs he cares for.) He then went off whistling in that manner of his which causeth the doves to take flight or block their ear-holes with the tips of their wings.

---

77   Food was often sold in taverns.

Sam, the blacksmith's boy, said that he had heard tell that it was a disagreement over who had been sitting on a certain stool first[78]. The guards in the barbican had three or four different versions of events but they all agreed on one thing: it was over the love of a woman.

I found myself thinking of Lady Gertrude again, and wondering whether I'd risk my life for her. Though my answer was yes, it would not be in a common tavern, but on the jousting field[79], wearing my lady's favour[80]. She maketh me feel all gooey inside.

---

78   Far more people sat on stools than chairs in medieval Britain, often three-legged ones. Many more chairs survive from the period, though, because they were better made so more valuable and better looked after.
79   You can find out about jousting on page 43.
80   A lady might give a token of some sort – perhaps a coloured scarf – to a knight who would wear it in tournament, for example, tied around his arm. This would be the lady's favour and show that he was dedicating his performance to her.

Martin interrupted my thoughts when his ample de Conk nose cast a shadow across my face, causing me to blink.

"Why do you have such a dreamy look upon your visage[81]?" he enquired.

"You were thinking of that Gertrude, were you not?" asked Cadwallon, stepping from the shadows. He moveth with the quietness of Mews, the castle cat, about to pounce on an unsuspecting dove when there are no easy rats to be had.

"I was NOT!" I lied.

"Then why does thou have the face of a soppy cow in Castle's Field[82]?" he demanded.

He had a point.

"I am thinking," I replied.

"That be a first," grinned Martin.

---

81 face
82 In times of unrest and of war, livestock could be brought inside the castle walls for safety as well as a food supply and, in the case of cows, milk. Horses were kept inside the castle compound whenever their owners were there. Protecting the horses – which made knights what later became thought of as 'the cavalry' – was a very important role of the castle.

Day 63

Today we rode forth from Widemoat Castle, the trees in leaf and spring flowers in the meadows. 'We' being Lord Widemoat's son and heir Sir William, Sir Jack Olde, Martin, Cadwallon and myself, along with an accompaniment of soldiers. Though these be times of peace, it is always best to be on guard, Sir Jack is always keen to remind us. The weather was fair, and the road not too rocky. Our destination? A monastery across the valley where we were to see monks at work, writing the scriptures[83]. We have no Bible at home but

---

83   Books were not printed in Europe in medieval times but
      handwritten. Most were religious books, by far the most common
      being the Bible.

Lord Widemoat hast one of which I have seen
a page or two. It is EXTRAORDINARY[84].
Martin professed to never having seen a
proper book. (It concerneth me that his ample
nose might require him to keep a certain
distance from the pages.) Cadwallon makes
out as if books are as plentiful as flies on bad
meat and it bores him to be going to see yet
another being written. Sometimes I do find him
so very hard to fathom.

---

84   Books written by monks were illuminated manuscripts: words
     embellished with decorations and pictures, often brightly coloured
     including gold.

The start of the journey was uneventful. We met few people on the way. Then, we heard the tinkling of a bell coming over the brow of a hill.

"Everyone halt," instructed Sir William with the tone of someone used to being obeyed without question.

We halted. I was on a horse named Lightning which, the truth be told, was about the only fast and exciting thing about him. A better name might have been Slug.

Martin was sharing a horse with Cadwallon, a fact which pleased neither of them. They had finally agreed that Cadwallon should ride them to the monastery with Martin holding on behind and that Martin should be in front upon the return journey. Their horse went by the name of Shank.

"Why have we stopped?" Martin asked Old Sir Jack Olde. (He would not think to ask Sir William Widemoat directly.)

"Did you not hear the bell?" asked our gnarled teacher.

"Why should we make way for an English

cow[85]?" asked Cadwallon, as though he were comparing one to a Welsh sheep or mountain goat, and found it lacking.

Sir William had obviously heard the scowling Welsh boy's words and turned to cast his eyes upon him. "Cow, is it?" he asked. "And what if it be not a cow but a leper?"

---

85   Cattle would sometimes wear bells around their necks

I shuddered at the word. Leprosy be the most terrible of afflictions, beginning with the loss of extremities such as fingers and toes[86]. The face can become so horribly disfigured that the poor victim looketh like the Devil himself on some painting of Hell on a chancel arch[87].

Sir William had already nodded to the lead guard in his escort who was now riding slowly ahead to discover the source of the ringing. We waited. My heart sounded as if it were beating in my ear.

When the guard returned from over the brow of the hill, he was accompanied by a most forlorn looking fellow. He was wearing a cap that drooped down either side of his head like the floppy ears of a most unhappy rabbit. Hanging from it, from a long thread was a single bell. The reason for our delay.

On seeing Lord Widemoat's son, the man

---

86   In medieval times it was feared that one could easily catch leprosy from a leper.

87   With so few people able to read, and Heaven and Hell seen as being very real, arches in front of the alter in many church were painted with terrible scenes of Hell as a warning to sinners.

snatched the cap from his head and bowed.

"And who might you be?" Sir William asked him, not unkindly.

"Mumble, Sire," he mumbled.

"And what brings you out upon the road to Widemoat, Mumble?"

"My destination is the castle, sire. I have heard that its master, Lord Widemoat, is a kind and generous man and I would wish to entertain him."

"You look more as if you might make him sad in your current disposition," said Sir William, and I was inclined to agree. I couldn't imagine poor Mumble bringing merriment and mirth to the great hall. He might fill the room with GLOOM.

"I did not set out this way," said Mumble, "but I was robbed."

Robbers! A look passed between me, Martin and Cadwallon.

"I am sorry to hear that," said Sir William, "for I am William Widemoat, heir to Widemoat Castle. I had hoped that our protection extended to the road."

Mumble clutched his cap more tightly and gave another bow, jingling as he did so. "An honour, sire," he said.

"What were you robbed of, Mumble?" Old Sir Jack asked.

"That is the oddest of most odd things, sire," Mumble replied. "They seized my knotted climbing-rope, and nothing more."

"But what can be so special about a rope?" asked a puzzled Sir William. I was wondering the same. Surely a rope is a rope is a rope?

"'Tis like no other rope, sire," said Mumble. "If it were, I would not have been able to carry it. Any ordinary rope of such length would be too large and cumbersome to carry about my person." He looked sad enough to have lost a friend. "This rope is not course and thick, but much narrower in dimensions and smoother on the hands. This makes it light, thin, easy to climb and to coil. Despite its great length, it was easy to store in my sack. It is – it *was* – the centrepiece of my act." His face, which had brightened for a moment at the thought of it, now fell again. "Now gone, along with my dignity."

"Who would want such a thing?" said Sir William.

"Who, indeed?" mutter Old Sir Jack Olde.

"I am known for my great feats of climbing and fear that they may be rival entertainers!" said Mumble.

Further questioning revealed that the wandering entertainer had been robbed a day since[88] near a crossroad, either side of which was deeply wooded, allowing robbers to remain hidden before and after their dirty deed was done.

It was decided that one of the guards would accompany Mumble to the castle whilst the remainder of us would continue our journey to the monastery as planned.

Such is the importance of Sir William that we were met at the abbey by none other than the Abbot himself. He is one of the roundest people I have ever laid eyes upon.

There is an old trick of getting rust off old armour by rolling it in a barrel of sand.

---

88   The day before/the previous day.

Abbot Chancery reminded me most of one such barrel! I almost wished he'd trip so that we might see if *he* rolled.

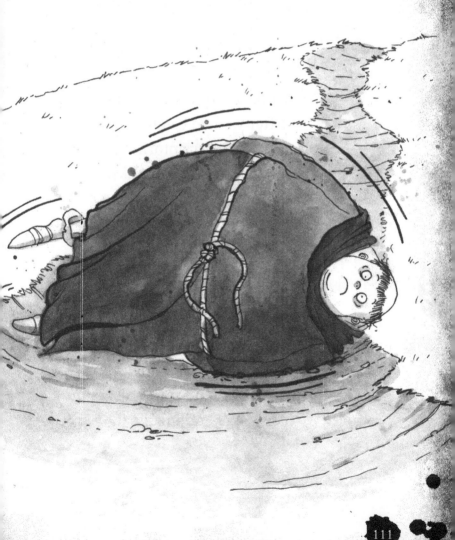

The Abbot offered us refreshment after our journey, which included small beer[89] for us pages. There was bread and some form of cheese. Martin slipped a piece beneath his shirt, no doubt saved to give to Rat, his rat. After we had eaten, the Abbot led us to the scriptorium: a room containing eight monks, all of whom were working at slopped writing desks, quill pens in hand.

Their writing was remarkable. A kind of magic. The letters and pictures glowed with life. It did not matter that I could not read more than a few words of the Latin, for each page was so beautiful... and it was all being produced by men's skill and imagination.

---

89   'Small beer' was weak beer, usually drunk by children. Few nobles would have drunk plain water.

The monks stopped work immediately when their abbot entered the room but Abbot Chancery said something -- I know not what – and the monks resumed their writing.

Although I hope one day to be the finest rider, archer, swordsman and lancer in the land, I know that I could never, in one thousand years, write in such away.

Before leaving, Sir William made a point of telling Abbot Chancery about Mumble being attacked. The monks need to be aware of robbers in the woods. Then we began our journey home, arriving back here at the castle before nightfall.

Preparing for bed in the Great Hall, Martin found all three of us a spot beside an already sleeping figure. Although his face was covered, I realised that the form was that of Tobias de Witt. How? Because he had removed his shoes before sleep and placed them by his trundle. I stared at them in the fading light.

Day 70

Rumours spread quickly in a castle, like the pox[90], with so many people working together in one place. And now the talk be of just one thing: the Welsh becoming restless. Some say that they are even gathering together their forces.

Today, in what little free time I had, I visited Fallow and the falcons. Though I may not get the chance to fly one, even in training, he taketh delight in my interest, and letteth me follow him as he works.

"What's in there?" I

---

90   The pox was the name for a number of viral diseases producing a rash of pimples that become pus-filled and leave pockmarks.

asked, pointing to a squat wooden building not unlike the others but fallen into disrepair.

"'Tis the old mews, abandoned before my time," said Fallow. "His Lordship cannot decide whether to pull it down or have it repaired."

When I stuck my head through the open doorway, I saw the large sack that I'd nearly tripped over that day. But now it had something inside it, causing it to bulge like the Abbot's belly. I was about to investigate, when I heard Cadwallon call my name.

"John!" he said. "We are to have extra weapons training! Sir Jack wanteth us now. The possibility of attack groweth by the day!"

Although part of me was afeared, I cannot deny that a shiver of excitement ran through me. I am a Drawbridge! We Drawbridges laugh in the face of danger.

HA!
HA!
HA!
HAAA!

Seest?

Day 74

Today, Old Sir Jack Olde says that if there
be a battle, as well as our having the trained
soldiers and knights on horseback, the men
who work on Lord Widemoat's land will act
as foot-soldiers – without proper armour or
any such – and their weapons can be anything
from rocks to hammers to farm tools. And
the yeomen will be called in to assist also as
archers. If you think a rock maketh a silly
weapon, you'll probably think again if you're
hit on the head with one… Once you wake up
with a thumping great headache.

Day 79

Since arriving at the castle, I have been trained in sword-fighting, most often with real swords and wooden shields. My opponent is usually Martin. Today, I managed to send his sword flying out of his hand. It missed Old Sir Jack by a goat's whisker.[91] Sir Jack did not know whether to shout at me and shake his fist or to shower me with praise for good swordsmanship... so he chose to do both.

I have also, of course, been learning how to charge with a lance against my confounded and most dastardly enemy, the quintain![92] And now, at last, I am the master of it.

No more bruises from that swinging sack!!!

Old Sir Jack Olde hath declared that I am ready to move on and practice jousting against a living, breathing opponent!

---

91   Goats DO have whiskers. They're just hard to see!
92   See page 43.

It hath truly
been a most
excellent day.

Day 81

It is with much

ANNOYANCE

that I must finally admit that Hubert hath become a good horseman, even if he is not quite so good as he boasteth he be.

As a squire, he is now used to riding with heavy armour on (his armour weigheth as much as a fat sheep) so hath built up his muscles, and is much stronger than the toothy-grinned layabout I remember lazing around at home. He hath proved this lately by lifting me up a great deal.

He did this today but I was ready for him. I flicked his ears until he put me down. He found it most annoying and called me some very rude names indeed.

Day 88

Today a squire – I remember not his name – spat at Cadwallon as he passed us in the courtyard. I saw Cadwallon clench his fist but he said nothing and did nothing in return. He simply looked down at the cobbles with his black, black eyes.

"Why doth he not like you?" I asked.

"It is not me he doth not like," said Cadwallon, "but the fact that I am Welsh."

This was most unfair, what with Cadwallon's father being on the side of our king.

If we were at war with people with big noses, I know who would have been spat upon instead.

Day 92

The atmosphere hath changed overnight. This morning, the castle is being readied.

For attack?
To attack?
For a battle?
For all-out war?

I know not. Peasants are already pouring through the main gate to be within the protection of the castle walls. Not an hour since, there was the clatter of hooves on wood as what few cattle there are were led across the bridge and past the raised portcullis and beneath the murder holes. Guards be lining the battlements, bristling with pikestaffs.

Some of us, including myself, Martin and Cadwallon, have been ordered to fill up buckets from the well[93] which we then distribute about the castle, hither and thither[94].

"Are these for the livestock to drink from?" I asked Sir Corbel, who was giving us orders. I watched the few remaining cows and sheep being led through the gate. Many looked better-fed than the peasants who brought them in.

"No, lad," he said. "These are to put out fires."

When I asked *what fires*, he bade me talk less and work faster.

Now, at the end of the day, my arms feel stretched and I have aches in places that I did not know I had places.

---

93 A supply of water was vital for any castle's location and had a big say when choosing a site to build on.
94 Here and there.

Day 95

Widemoat Castle hath been in a state of readiness for a few days now. The waiting hath been most terrible, even for those of us who are not sure exactly what we are waiting for. A scouting party of ten knights and their squires – totalling twenty – all on horseback rode forth yesterday.

All Old Sir Jack Olde would tell us was that they were "seeing the lie of the land". I do not think he meant the humps and bumps and hillocks and tufts of grass, but rather the state of things between us English and the Welsh. But I cannot be sure. Everyone is being careful what they say. It is clear that Lord Widemouth hath given the instruction that, with few exceptions, each of us only needs to know his part in the plan and not the over-all scheme of things.

My brother Hubert rode out with Sir Richard Kitchen. I know he is a terrible brother AND an idiot. But he is my brother and I pray God keep him safe.

Day 97

I was awoken in the night by Hubert shaking my shoulder. He is alive! He looked dirty and exhausted.

"The Welsh are coming, Little Brother," he whispered.

I struggled into a sitting position, about to speak.

He put his finger to his lips.

"Shhh now," he said. "You must be brave, John, and do father and mother proud. How we behave these next days or weeks will reflect upon the Drawbridge family name."

I found my chest filling with pride. Even Hubert looked different. Perhaps it was the light cast from the stubby candle he carried, but something made him look more dignified. Less of an idiot. More like a man on the way to becoming a knight.

Day 98

Today, the drawbridge be up and the portcullis be down. There be a goodly selection of small but painful items ready to be dropped through the murder holes. Chicken poo won't do against real enemies. There is an atmosphere of much tension and suspense. Even Doug the kennel boy has stopped his tuneless whistling that usually so annoyeth Charles the minstrel. The ladies[95] have been ordered to remain within two rooms in the keep, for their own safety.

---

95   The ladies would have been Lady Widemoat's youngest daughters, along with those young ladies sent from elsewhere to be trained by her, and the wives of the knights.

Day 99

I am greatly shocked and so very angry.

CADWALLON HATH BEEN LOCKED IN A ROOM IN ONE OF THE TOWERS!!!

Well, not *locked* precisely but he hath been confined there. Yes, he frowneth and muttereth a great deal, and yes, he is Welsh, but he has not spoken so much as one word in favour of the rebels supposedly upon their way.

This is even MORE unfair than my older brother being older than me! And that is one of the great injustices of all time.

Fumeth

It was the steward, Merrick, who took Cadwallon to the tower, not a soldier, but I still reckon Cadwallon to be a prisoner in anything but name! I asked Old Sir Jack Olde if HE could do anything.

"It is as much for your young friend's good as anything," he responded. "You have seen how many look at him with mistrust."

Friend, he had said. It was then it occurred to me that, yes, I suppose Cadwallon is my friend. Not in the way that Martin and I hath become friends, but friends all the same.

"You think some here might harm him, Sir Jack?" I asked

"You've seen how some of the servants and soldiers look at him and talk about him behind his back," said Sir Jack. "They think him a spy or, at least, a viper in the nest. If things turn bad then they may turn bad for Cadwallon too!"

I understand what
Sir Jack meant, but
I still think it unfair.
And even I am
not allowed to see
Cadwallon. If it were
Martin de Conk
who was prisoner,
he could stick his
nose out of the tower
window and I could
climb up it…

Day 100

The first we knew of the advancing enemy was when a cry went up from those on the battlements of the barbican. The Welsh had been sighted! I was helping Oats feed the horses when the warning was sounded. I think I shall never forget the feeling in the pit of my stomach: a mixture of real fear mixed with a tingle of excitement. A look of sadness passed like a wave across Old Sir Jack's weathered features.

"So it begins," he said with a sigh.

Less than two hours' later, a large force had amassed at the front of the castle.

Day 103

It hath been an exhausting past few days. And I thank God that Widemoat Castle hath such a wide moat. Without the moat, the Welsh could have rolled a siege tower right up to the outer wall: a huge wooden tower filled with enemy soldiers, protecting them from our defence from the battlements. They would then have been the right height to swarm out and over the top of the wall. But the moat stopped any such siege tower reaching us.

Another common trick to overcome the defences of a castle is to tunnel beneath a wall – Old Sir Jack told us that the best place be a point of weakness such as the corner of a tower, say – holding up said tunnel with wooden props. When complete, the enemy could then set a fire within, burning the props and causing the tunnel and the wall above to collapse… resulting a breach in castle defences through which the attackers could pour. Try that at Widemoat, however, and the Welsh would have to get across the moat before tunnelling and, most likely, end up with a half-hearted tunnel full of foul-smelling water…

So what do we have to worry about? A great deal, as we soon discovered. I had, of course heard of catapults but when the rebelling Welsh forces rolled one into position with a rousing cheer, I marvelled at the size of it. A wooden frame on wheels, it had a fixed firing arm tied down and ready to be released…

…and then I saw the slingshot catapult, sometimes called the trebuchet. I gasped out loud.

It was EVEN bigger.
It was EVEN taller.

It looked even more dangerous, with a loose sling hanging from the end.

Orders were given to the castle archers to make the soldiers operating these catapults their main targets but, as well as their armour, many were protected by large wicker shields as tall as small walls.

Arrows rained down from out battlements as the slingshot was loaded with a large boulder that took many a Welshman to lift.

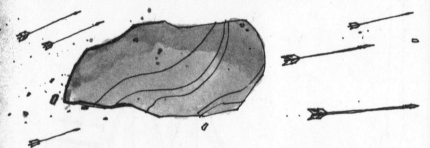

Meanwhile, those around the other catapult seemed to be loading it with anything and everything, including what appeared to be the carcass of a dead sheep.

"How do they hope to break thick stone walls with such ammunition?" Martin pondered.

"It's not the castle they be aiming for, boy," said an archer. "Those rocks and the like are meant for us."

I, for one, fancied not the idea of being flattened and splattered by a sheep, dead or otherwise.

I will never forget the sound of those catapults being released and the fear as their loads headed castlewards.

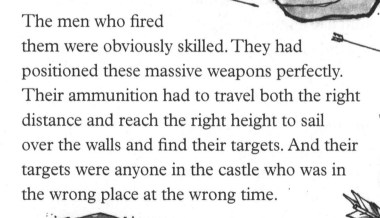

The men who fired them were obviously skilled. They had positioned these massive weapons perfectly. Their ammunition had to travel both the right distance and reach the right height to sail over the walls and find their targets. And their targets were anyone in the castle who was in the wrong place at the wrong time.

Although many of our enemy were killed or wounded, attacked with an endless onslaught of our arrows from above, their catapults caused death and injury also.

I later learned that one of our first number to be killed was Doug the kennel boy, which saddened me greatly.

I felt guilty at being annoyed by his whistling now that I knew I would hear it no more.

An earlier rock had split open the kennels, causing much fear amongst the hounds and, when trying to round them up and comfort them, a second rock had landed and crushed him like a bug underfoot.

I then found out the reason for the buckets we had placed. From a rocky outcrop, enemy archers were attempting to fire burning arrows up and into the castle. And some found their mark.

Soon straw and wooden structures in the castle courtyard were alight but not ablaze. Not ablaze because any man or boy without a weapon in his hand was forming a human chain of water-filled buckets, extinguishing such flames before they took hold…

…which is why I am now sooty and exhausted as both sides have fallen silent for the night.

Day 104

More of the same.

Attacked.

Defended.

More missiles.

More fires.

More injuries.

Day 105

It is now the strong suspicion in Widemoat Castle that the Welsh rebels are not alone in their rebellion and have some disgruntled English folk amongst their number. How else could they have such large and modern weaponry as those? I wish we could ride out and attack, having knight face knight as at the lists[96] during a tournament.[97] Instead, we wait.

---

96 An enclosed area for a tournament
97 A trial of skills between knights involving jousting or 'tilting' with a lance and, once knocked off their horses, fighting with sword, mace and morning star on foot.

Day 109

Such excitement and treachery in
the night! It was my plan to pay a
visit to Cadwallon when all else
were asleep. I had hidden a
candle away for just such
a purpose, to light my way.
I awoke to discern from the
moonlight through a gap in
the shutters that Martin was no
longer asleep on his trundle beside

mine! His ample nose creates a most distinctive
silhouette that was now absent from my view.
Had he a similar plan to see Cadwallon? If so,
why had he not told me? Then again, I had not
told him either!

I carefully picked a path through the hundred or so forms of snoring, muttering and shifting sleeping men and made it to the Great Hall door and slipped out into the passageway. (Such is the snoring at night, I am convinced the pigs would complain about the noise if their sty were nearby.)

There was a torch alight in the passage, from which I lit my candle. Although the castle was heavily guarded upon the outside, with soldiers posted along the battlements, most facing the camped-out rebels at the front, inside the castle there was little evidence of extra soldiers on duty.

I was making my way to the tower when I heard the squeaking of a rat. There be nothing that unusual in such a sound, though the more sensible rats confine themselves to the kitchen or stores where food is more likely to be found. But then I heard a voice.

"Keep that thing quiet!" it whispered. "Do you want us discovered?"

I knew then that whoever was talking was talking to Martin about Rat. But whose voice was it?

I crept closer, planning to give them a mighty surprise. Perhaps even make them jump out of their own skins! I grinned.

Then the voice spoke again. "We have little time," it said. "The signal hath be sent. We must lower the rope. Keep lookout!"

A cold shiver passed through my body. This was the voice of Tobias de Witt. And then I realised where I stood: outside the garderobe from which I found Martin emerging after my day of falconry. The day Martin had stayed behind saying he was ill. The one garderobe that stood out from all the other garderobes because it did not have a protective grill to… to prevent the enemy from *climbing up it*.

Then I caught sight of an empty sack upon the floor. The bulging sack of which I'd caught a glimpse within the abandoned mews. It must have contained Mumble's stolen rope. The rope they were about to lower!

My heart began to beat like Magnus's hammer upon his blacksmith's anvil. I blew out my candle. A moment later, I could just make out Martin's head poking through the doorway; his nose sticking out like the gnomon of a sundial[98]. He was holding a sword, resting the point on the ground.

What to do?!? I knew that I must act before it was too late!

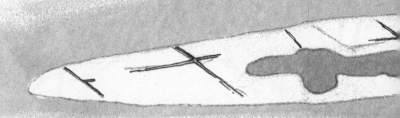

---

98   Sundials, water clocks and marked candles were the most common types of clock in the middle ages. The gnomon is the sticking-up part of the sundial that casts its time-telling shadow in sunlight.

A thousand-and-one ideas – well, a handful – flashed through my mind at once. I could rush into the room, knock de Witt to the ground and somehow wedge him in the hole to prevent the soldiers from getting in ...

...or run down to the kitchen and get a tray of hot fat from beneath the spit and bring it up and tip it through the hole onto the up-coming enemy...

…or, once I had somehow removed Martin and de Witt from the scene, wait for each soldier to climb up through the hole in turn, knock him unconscious, then wait for the next one and do the same…

…or simply run and get help. And what if I was caught along the way? What if these two were not acting alone?

I thought of the rope.

I remembered the sword held loosely in Martin's hand.

I had the element of surprise upon my side.

Before Martin knew what was happening, I charged him in the dark, pushing him backward with great force and snatching the sword at the same time. He fell back into the room with a "Wha--?!" startling Tobias de Witt who was peering down the hole of the toilet, a small guttering candle stuck to the wooden seat with melted wax, giving off a little light.

Before he fully realised what was happening, I charged him with sword raised, shouting,

as loud as my lungs would allow. This was both in an attempt to frighten him somewhat and attract the attention of others.

Tobias de Witt raised his arms to defend himself but he was not my target. I brought the blade down on the rope which was tied to an iron grille in a window, the other end disappearing down the chute. The rope was thin and taught, and the blade sharp and heavy. It cut through with one hack of the sword. I heard a cry, followed soon after by further cries and some muffled splashes. More than one rebel must have been climbing up that rope at a time.

Martin had now struggled to his feet and Tobias de Witt had had time to think. They both turned on me but, with the rope gone, this part of their plan, at least, lay in tatters.

As they approached, I held out my sword before me. Tobias was unarmed and Martin only had his nose, but it was still two against one.

"Hardly a fair fight," said a voice from the doorway. Never in my whole life was I so pleased to see Hubert, MY MAGNIFICENT BIG BROTHER.

Day 110

Today has been a clear and sunny day which brought with it reinforcements. You should have seen the rebel forces scatter like ants fleeing a big foot in a large boot, when a small army of knights and foot-soldiers came swarming down the hill to attack the attackers.

"Who is that leading them?" I asked a soldier at the battlements, look down upon a man with no helmet and flowing black hair, riding a white horse bare-back.

"'Tis none other than Rhodri Llewelyn!" he cried.

A cheer went up around the castle and, as those rebels not killed or wounded fled, Cadwallon was being carried shoulder-high to the top of the highest tower for the best view. For Rhodri Llewelyn is his father.

Soon the fight was over before it was really begun. But think how differently things might have been had Martin and Tobias succeeded. I smiled to myself.

In the light of day, their plan had become clear. Under the cover of darkness, rebel soldiers had taken a raft – which, by day, looked very much like just another one of their huge defensive wicker shields -- across the moat to where they waited out of view of those on the battlements. The stolen knotted rope was then lowered from the garderobe and their intention was to climb into the castle and make their way to the gatehouse, where they would overpower our soldiers and lower the drawbridge to let their army overrun the castle. Such fiends!

But we put a stop to that.

$$\underline{\underline{\frac{I-yes}{ME\ ME}}}$$

ME – put a stop to that.

Much *yah-boo-sucks*-ing and sticking out of tongues!!!

If I were to glow any more with pride, I think I would become hotter than a spit boy![99]

---

99 Spit boys were not boys but grown men. Theirs was the 'lowest' job in the kitchen: to turn the huge joints of meat on an iron spit in front of a huge fire. This was exhausting work. They would often have to turn the spit for six or so hours, without a break, for the meat to cook. And, standing so close to the fire themselves, they would have become almost unbearably hot – almost cooked! – themselves.

When brought before Lord Widemoat himself, flanked by knights and soldiers, Tobias de Witt and Martin De Conk were forced to explain their actions.

"Why betray us in this manner?" demanded the lord.

Tobias de Witt spoke first. "Why?" he blurted out. "Why? My father was killed in a tavern and, as you well know, the man who killed him was none other than the brother to your own steward, Merrick! And no action was ever taken against him." He spat upon the floor, narrowly missing his most distinctive footwear.

A guard went to strike him with an iron-clad hand.

Lord Widemoat raised his own hand as a signal not to do so. "Tobias," he said. His voice not unkind. "I am familiar with these events and sorry for the loss of your father, but Merrick's brother, the man who killed him was acting in self-defence and, even if he were not, this is no excuse for treachery."

I felt saddened, from my place in the side-lines, seeing Martin – bowed and defeated – brought before His Lordship in this way. What had he been thinking?

"And what of you, Master de Conk?" asked

Lord Widemoat. "What is your reason for such betrayal?"

Martin raised his head, his nose pointing skyward like the beak of a baby bird waiting to be fed. "My family is one of the oldest and finest in the land. The first de Conk on English soil came over with the Conqueror himself[100]. Yet how are we talked about today? For our valiant deeds? For our loyalty to the crown[101]?

---

100 William the Conqueror, who came with armies from Normandy in 1066, defeated King Harold and became what the historians generally agree the first king of all England.

101 The king.

No, for the bigness of our noses."

"Well, they ARE big," said Lord Widemouth.

"Enormous, if yours be anything to go by," muttered the guard.

"Massive," muttered another.

Martin glared. "So my father decided that, when I was sent here to train as a page, we might join forces with the rebels and strike a blow for the de Conks!"

The first de Conk

"A *nose* blow[102]?" suggested the Fool stepping out from beside His Lordship's chair, waving his pig's bladder on a stick. And his grin *was* even greater than my own.

---

102 Very few people had handkerchiefs back then, but King Richard II is credited with having invented them.

Lord Widemoat failed to suppress a laugh and raised an eyebrow in a fashion most comical. He nodded towards Martin and de Witt. "Take them away," he said.

Poor Martin was led from His Lordship's presence with laughter ringing in his ears. Proof, if proof were needed, that hundreds of years of name-calling can have consequences. There can be cruelty in words and a part of me felt bad for the page I had thought of as a friend.

Day 118

Over the past week, even more information hath come to light. Martin's paper, on which he had written

referred not to the castle cat by name, but to the falconry barn. Why did I not think of it before? I am more of a fool than I thought I be! The mews was a place where, at certain times, he and Tobias could meet away from prying eyes. After all, it was there that Tobias had hidden the rope after stealing it from poor Mumble with the help of a few Welsh outsiders. He confessed to smuggling the stolen rope into the castle hidden amongst provision for his cousin, Alan de Witt, the guards at the gate none the wiser.

As for Martin trying to squeeze through the portcullis that day, perhaps he had been practicing for some evil deed, rather than simply having fun? And to think all of this was going on under my (much smaller and better-looking) nose. Martin was more of a rat than Rat his rat!

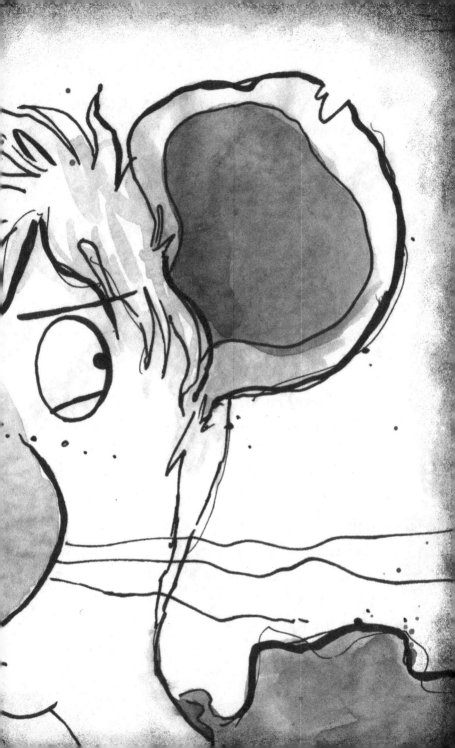

With the siege ended, the enemy defeated and two weeks passed, a tournament is in progress to celebrate Widemoat Castle's victory. What is more,

I be the <u>HERO</u>
of the hour.

I have never known the gap-toothed Hubert to be so proud to be my brother (a fact which he keepeth reminding anyone and everyone of). And, truth be told, I am proud of him. Cadwallon's father is guest of honour, and sitteth beside Lord Widemoat as the first joust begineth. It is between Hubert's knight, Sir Richard Kitchen and the loathsome Sir Theobold Oakwood who tripped me that day just for the fun of it...

… and, YES! It be his turn to take a tumble. Sir Richard hath just unseated him from his horse with his lance at first attempt. The crowd cheereth but none cheereth louder than me! I see the Lady Gertrude look over to me and smile. I blush and Cadwallon elboweth me in the ribs and grinneth, dark eyes flashing.

I love Widemoat Castle.

I could not be happier.

There be no place on this Earth that I would rather be.

And here John Drawbridge
ended his secret diary.

AND
NEXT...?

John Drawbridge did, indeed, go on to become a squire and, over time, a knight. He was known for his bravery and kind and chivalrous behaviour to people in all walks of life. He married a certain Lady Gertrude Pikestaff – a few years older than himself – and they had eleven children: ten girls and one boy, whom they named Douglas but called 'Doug' after someone they both once knew. If Sir John had one fault, it was that – for some strange reason – he always had an irrational and unfair mistrust of people with large noses. His favourite part of any castle remained the drawbridge.

A NOTE FROM THE AUTHOR

ONLY
THE
FACTS
ARE TRUE

Although none of the characters in this book are real and there is and was no Widemoat Castle, there was indeed often unrest between the English and the Welsh, though it may not have erupted in quite the way it did in John Drawbridge's diary. What IS true is the information about castles, the types of people who lived in them and their daily lives. Another great way to bring history to life is, of course, to visit a National Trust castle. It's probably best not to take a real sword with you, though. Or, come to think of it, a knotted rope or pet rat.

Philip Ardagh

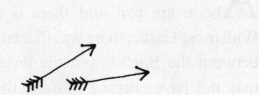